Where's my Mummy?

PIPPBROOK
BOOKS

It was another sunny day down on the farm.

One baby chick, a funny little fellow,
fluffy and wide-eyed, perfectly yellow,
stretched and yawned and looked around –
but Mummy Hen was nowhere to be found.

Was she out with the sheep, munching on the grass?

"BAAA!" said the sheep. "Your mummy's not here, but don't be sad — she must be near."

"Oh dear," said the chick, and he shook his head. "I'd better look somewhere else instead."

BAAA

Was she rolling in the mud with the big pink pig?

"OINK!" said the pig. "Mud's the place for me –
but squishing and squelching's
just for piggies, you see!"

OINK!

"Oh dear," said the chick, and he shook his head.
"I'd better look somewhere else instead."

OINK!

Was she hiding in the milk shed with the farmer's favourite cow?

"MOO!" said the cow. "I'm sorry my dear, but if she can't be milked you'll not find her here."

"Oh dear," said the chick, and he shook his head. "I'd better look somewhere else instead."

MOO!

Was she on the
rooftop, calling
"Cock-a-doodle-doo"?

"No" said the cockerel.
"She's not up here with me."
"Oh dear," cheeped the chick.
"Well, where can Mummy be?"

COCK-A-DOODLE-DOO!

"CHEEP, CHEEP!"
cried the chick,
with a tear in his eye.
"If I don't find her soon,
I might start to cry."

Then around the corner
who should come,
with a **CLUCK, CLUCK, CLUCK,**
but the little chick's mum!

"Where have you been?"
Mummy Hen cried.
"I've been all around the farm,
searching far and wide."

But before her chick could answer,
she clutched him to her breast,
and took him safely home,
to their lovely, cosy nest.